Squishy McFluff

The Invisible Cat

Seaside Rescue!

For Ava and Ruby, sunshine girls!
And with huge thanks to my dream team: Julia,
Leah, Rebecca, Hannah, Susan, Emma, Will
and, of course, Ella. Xx

First published in 2016
by Faber and Faber Limited
Bloomsbury House
74–77 Great Russell Street
London WC1B 3DA

Designed by Faber and Faber
Printed in Europe

A CIP record for this book is available from the British Library

978–0571–32068–4

2 4 6 8 10 9 7 5 3 1

Squishy McFluff
The Invisible Cat

Seaside Rescue!

by *Pip Jones*

Illustrated by *Ella Okstad*

ff

FABER & FABER

Can you see him? My kitten?

His long whiskers shimmer!

He's so good at digging

(but he's not a good swimmer).

Imagine him, quick!

Have you imagined enough?

Oh good! You can see him!

It's Squishy McFluff!

As the sun rose one morning,

at the end of July,

And fluffy clouds drifted

across the blue sky,

Ava danced round her room,

shouting: 'Hip, hip, hooray!

'It's **holiday** time!

And we're going TODAY!'

Mum packed the clothes,

   Baby Roo packed a teddy,

While Dad said (repeatedly):

   'Are we all ready?!'

Ava waited and waited,

among all her stuff,

With her invisible kitten,

Squishy McFluff.

At last, they set off,

all so happy and merry,

Loading the car and then

boarding a ferry.

Their holiday started at

quarter to three,

When they dropped off their bags

and went straight to the sea.

Ava arranged all her

buckets and spades.

Mum had a parasol,

Dad wore his shades,

And Roo, as she chomped on

the grains in her hand,

Pulled a face when she realised

you shouldn't eat sand!

Well, far too excited

to lounge in the sun,

Ava said: 'Squishy!

Let's go and have fun!'

'Er, suncream!' called Mum.

'You don't want to get fried!'

'But Squishy HATES suncream,'

Ava replied.

'The pong makes him sneeze!

His fur gets all sticky!'

'Admittedly,' Mum said,

'it would be quite tricky

'To put suncream on

an invisible cat . . .

'But you NEED it, Ava.

The sun's hot. That's that.'

Ava huffed. Mum carefully

rubbed in the lotion,

Then Ava and Squish

scampered off to the ocean.

13

Enjoying the feel of the beach,

soft and damp,

Ava lifted her knees up,

and started to stamp!

She made monster footprints,

her toes widely splaying . . . !

But then Ava noticed that

Squish wasn't playing.

15

But of course! What a shame.

Poor Squishy McFluff!

Oh, he tried . . . but he just wasn't

heavy enough!

16

So, using four pebbles

and one little shell,

Ava carefully drew him

some footprints as well.

'What next?' Ava asked,

when they'd finished their stroll.

Squish patted the sand to say,

'Let's dig a HOLE!'

'Yippee!' cried Ava.

'Squish, you use your paw

'And I'll use my spades.

　　We might reach the earth's core!

'If we dig really deep,

　　we could get to Australia!'

So, with all sorts of digging

　　paraphernalia,

They dug and they dug,

without any cares,

Flinging sand towards people

in stripy deckchairs.

'Hey!' said a lady.

An old chap yelled: 'STOP!'

As golden sand fell

on his big lollypop.

But Ava and Squishy,

they just kept on going.

The big hole got deeper,

the sand piles kept growing,

'Til one snoozing couple

got quite a surprise,

To find themselves buried

right up to their eyes!

After digging for forty-five

minutes or more,

Ava's hand began hurting,

as did McFluff's paw.

'We've done **very** well,' Ava said,

'with our crater,

'But maybe we'll look for

Australia later.'

Both so exhausted

from digging their trough,

Squish had a great thought

for how to cool off.

A magnificent plan!

It would work like a dream!

He (silently) miaowed

to tell Ava his scheme . . .

Across the hot beach,

both laughing and leaping,

Ava and Squish ran to Dad

(who was sleeping).

'Um, Dadd-ddy,' said Ava,

ever so sweetly,

'It's AWFULLY hot,

and poor Squishy's completely

'Sweaty and faint! He can't swim,

he might drown!

'So he can't just go into

the sea to cool down.'

'He needs something else . . .'

Ava whined. Daddy sighed.

'He'll get ILL if we don't

    try to help!' Ava cried.

'It's TERRIBLY hard

    having fur when it's sunny . . .'

Dad rolled his eyes –

    then gave Ava some money.

'Yum!' Ava squealed,

and they turned tail and ran

As fast as they could

to the big ice-cream van.

While a boy stood there waiting

for change from a pound,

McFluff clambered into

the van to look round.

Leaning in, Ava said:

'Has he got raspberry sauce?

'Some chocolate flakes too?

And some sprinkles, of course!'

The ice-cream man saw her and,

scratching his chin,

Said: 'Who are you talking to?

Hey, who snuck in?'

'Erm . . . it's my cat,'

Ava sheepishly muttered.

'Quivering whiskers!'

the ice-cream man spluttered.

'A CAT? In my VAN?

Quick, call him back!

'It's against health and safety!

They'll give me the sack!

'Where is he?'

The angry man's face had gone red.

So, pointing her finger,

Ava helpfully said:

'Behind you, behind you!

Mind where you stand!

'He's right by your shoe!

Now he's sniffing your hand!

'He's jumped on your shoulder!

His tail's in your EAR!

'Look harder! Turn quicker!

No, not THERE . . . he's here!'

Well, seeking the kitten

    (who could never be seen),

The man accidentally

    bumped the machine.

It buzzed into life,

    the big nozzle whirling,

And out of the spout

    lots of ice-cream came swirling.

With no cones to catch it,

   it dropped to the floor.

It had almost reached up

   to the ceiling before

The ice-cream man noticed

   and (panicking) slammed

His hand on the switch –

   but it was frozen and jammed!

The ice-cream kept coming.

The big machine chugged.

Out of the window

the sweet mixture glugged.

The ice-cream man shrieked,

and passers-by gaped

As the poor chap leapt clear

of the tide . . . and escaped.

Not sure **what** to do,

or quite what she could say,

Ava just passed him

her money to pay.

And, as sprinkles and cones

floated silently past,

She got her mouth-watering

ice-cream at last!

Off to the rock pools

the pesky pair trotted,

To see if some crabs

and shrimps might be spotted.

Ava paddled and kicked,

flicking water at Squish,

But then McFluff saw . . .

AN INVISIBLE FISH!

With a beautiful, wispy,

invisible tail,

It twinkled from every

invisible scale.

Squish just couldn't help it,

he swiped at its fin . . .

Then that clumsy invisible

kitten FELL IN!

Squishy scrambled and splashed

to climb on to a rock,

While Ava shrieked: 'SQUIIIIISH!'

– and, oh dear, what a shock

When a wave swept him off,

too far out to reach,

And he started . . . drifting . . .

away . . . from the beach.

As luck would have it,

    a bottle was bobbing

Right there in the ocean,

    so Ava yelled (sobbing):

'Climb on to the bottle!

    Hold on **very** tight!

'I'll go and get help, Squishy.

    You'll be alright!'

She watched as she sprinted

the length of the bay

But McFluff floated further

and further away . . .

Ava ran to her parents.

She was oh, SO upset

At the thought of McFluff

so lost and so wet.

'Just try to imagine him back!'

Daddy groaned.

'I can't! He has GONE!'

Ava wailed and she moaned.

'My poor little kitten!

He's so funny and clever,

'Oh, what will I DO

if I've lost him forever?'

'Hush now,' said Mummy,

'stop crying, don't worry.

'I know we can find him.

Let's look, come on, hurry!

'Squishy's so special to you –

  and, as such,

'He just can't stay lost,

  'cos you love him too much.'

With that, they set off,

  and Mum rented a boat

Which she dragged down the beach

  'til it started to float.

Determined to track down

McFluff for her daughter,

Mum began rowing out

over the water.

The waves crashed and rolled,

in huge frothy peaks.

Sea water and sweat trickled

over Mum's checks.

The rowing was hard work!

The sea was so rough.

'Can you see him?' Mum asked

(with a grunt and a puff).

Scanning the sparkling waters,

and squinting,

Ava said: 'Look, THERE!

I see something glinting!'

And so, pleased that the journey

was almost complete,

Mum heaved even harder

in the blistering heat.

Approaching the island,

Mum pushed on an oar

To steer the boat in

to the sandy white shore.

And just down the beach,

very soggy and flat,

Was Ava's bedraggled,

invisible cat!

Ava ran to him shouting:

'Oh, Squishy! I'm here!'

She knelt down beside him

and tickled his ear,

Then pulled on his tail,

and ruffled his fur.

McFluff's back paws twitched . . .

and he started to stir.

Squishy's eyes slowly opened . . .

and what a delight!

He leapt up to Ava,

and she hugged him so tight.

Then Mum, from the shade of

a tumble-down shack,

Said (with a big yawn):

'Right, shall we go back?'

Back safe and sound,

the sun low in the sky,

Mum said to her daughter:

'Could you both try

'To be good? And stay safe?

All this week? Please?'

Ava nodded and then gave her

Mummy a squeeze.

'And if Squish craves
invisible fish again later,
Don't try to catch one,
we'll just ask the waiter.'

McFluff (silently) miaowed

    to agree, but meanwhile . . .

    . . . Alone in the twilight,

    on a far away isle,

A thin, bearded man

    softly sighed as he found

Something familiar,

    by his feet, on the ground.

A battered old bottle,

washed up with the tide,

And UTTERLY empty.

There was nothing inside.

The very next morning

    (having dug a NEW hole),

Ava and Squish saw

    Sea Rescue Patrol

Arrive with a man,

    who looked weary and thin,

With a scruffy and scraggly

    beard on his chin.

'Look, Squish!' said Ava.

'He was rescued, like you!'

'Oh crumpets! I wonder

how anyone knew

'He was lost and just waiting,

alone, to be saved.'

Ava grinned at the man,

who smiled back and waved . . .

But he never would know

how the note he had written

Had managed to save

one invisible kitten.